The Little Manatee ©

www.TheLittleManatee.com

Printed in the USA

The Little Manatee©

These are facts about manatees.

The manatee is an endangered species.

There are only about 6,200 in Florida waters.

They are aquatic mammals like the Seal and Dolphin.

They are grey and have thick skin.

Manatees can grow up to 15 feet long.

They can weigh up to 3500 pounds!

The manatee is completly harmless and defenseless.

Please be alert and cautious in manatee areas when boating.

One bright and sunny day the Manatee family was
eating breakfast at one of their favorite places.
It was a safe area to be in and had lots of green
plants to eat.
After breakfast, the Little Manatee went exploring.

As the Little Manatee was swimming and exploring, he was scared by a boat that came very close to him.

3

He swam away from the boat as fast as he could.
He remembered what his parents had taught him,
not to swim close to any boats!

The Little Manatee looked around and realized
he was lost.

"Maybe I should have told my parents I was going
exploring," he thought to himself.
"They always taught me to ask for permission
before I go anywhere by myself,"
he thought to himself.

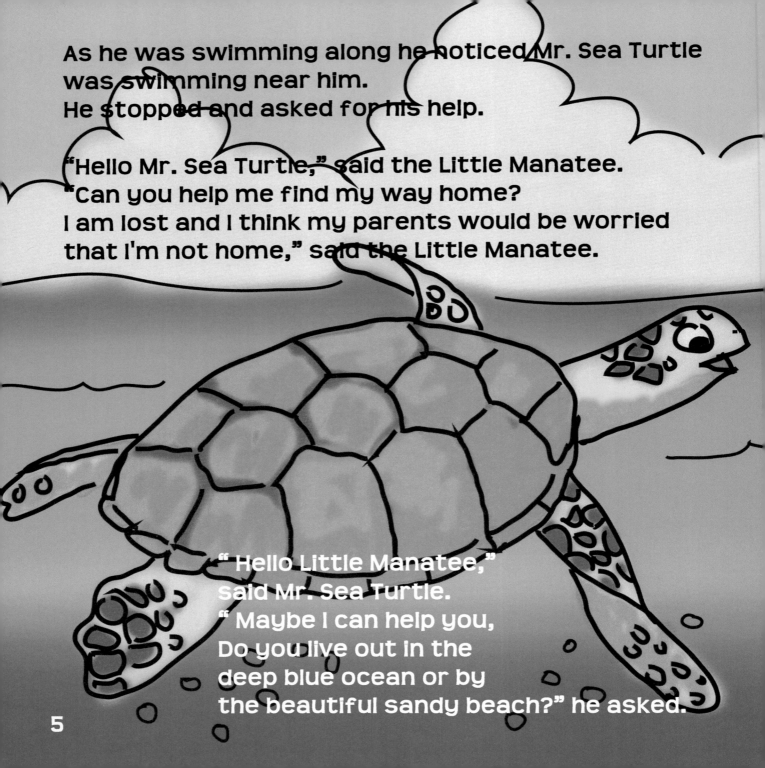

As he was swimming along he noticed Mr. Sea Turtle
was swimming near him.
He stopped and asked for his help.

"Hello Mr. Sea Turtle," said the Little Manatee.
"Can you help me find my way home?
I am lost and I think my parents would be worried
that I'm not home," said the Little Manatee.

" Hello Little Manatee,"
said Mr. Sea Turtle.
" Maybe I can help you,
Do you live out in the
deep blue ocean or by
the beautiful sandy beach?" he asked.

5

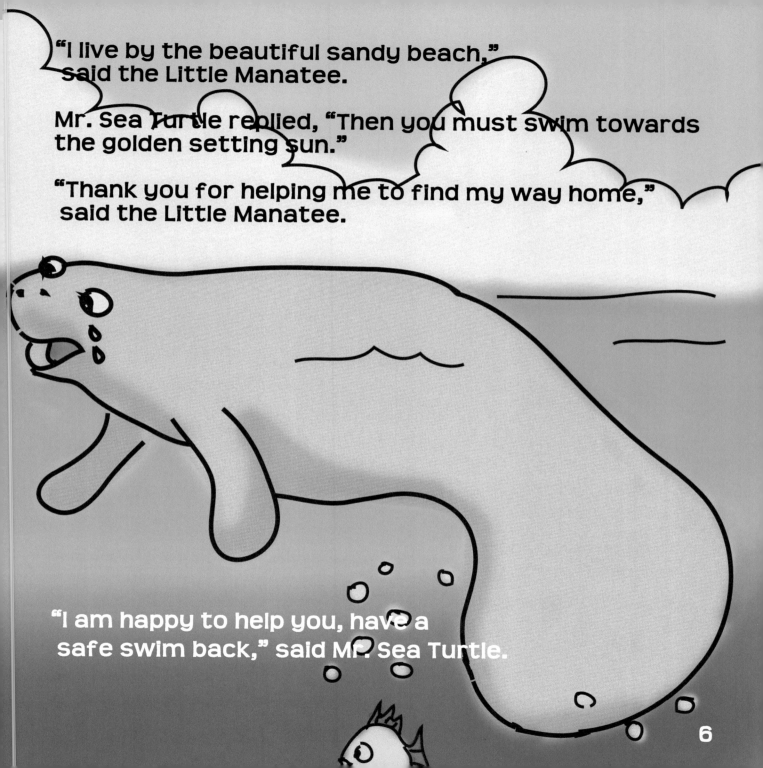

"I live by the beautiful sandy beach," said the Little Manatee.

Mr. Sea Turtle replied, "Then you must swim towards the golden setting sun."

"Thank you for helping me to find my way home," said the Little Manatee.

"I am happy to help you, have a safe swim back," said Mr. Sea Turtle.

6

As the Little Manatee was swimming back home.
He saw what looked like a shark!

"What if the shark will not let me swim past him?
I am so scared!" he said to himself.

He swam slowly closer towards the shark. He hoped
the shark was friendly.

As he got closer he realized...

... It was only Mr. and Mrs. Sea Dolphin.
He knew they were friendly.

"Hello Mr. and Mrs. Sea Dolphin,"
said the Little Manatee.
"Can you tell me if I am getting close to
the beach?" he asked.

"I have been lost all day and know
my parents will be worried where
I might be," said the Little Manatee.

"Oh yes, you must be the Little Manatee who has been missing. I met your parents over there by the big red lighthouse," said Mrs. Sea Dolphin. " They have been looking everywhere for you."

"If you go towards the big red lighthouse," said Mr. Sea Dolphin "you will find your parents there."

"Thank you so much! " said the Little Manatee. "I better hurry so my parents can stop worrying about me," he thought to himself.

As the Little Manatee got closer to the lighthouse, he noticed that there were three lighthouses. A blue one, a red one and a yellow one.

"Oh my," said the Little Manatee.
"Now what color lighthouse did Mr. Sea Dolphin tell me to swim towards?"

It must be the red one because it is in line with the golden setting sun.

The Little Manatee swam toward the red lighthouse as fast as he could. As a matter of fact, he never swam faster in his whole life!

Soon he saw his parent's right in front of him. "Mom, Dad," he shouted as loud as he could! "I'm home, I'm finally home," he said with joy!

Momma Manatee and Poppa Manatee turned around to see if that was their Little Manatee doing all the shouting.

13

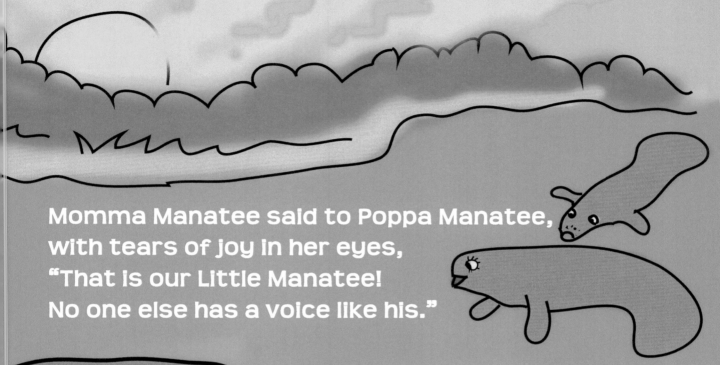

Momma Manatee said to Poppa Manatee,
with tears of joy in her eyes,
"That is our Little Manatee!
No one else has a voice like his."

They swam towards him feeling
so happy he was safe once again,
but they also were upset because
he did not tell them he was going
anywhere that morning.

14

"Mom, Dad," said the Little Manatee. "I'm sorry I did not ask for permission to go exploring by myself this morning. I will never do that again. I will always ask you both for permission before I go anywhere by myself, I was so scared!" he said.

His parents hugged and kissed him. "We hope this has taught you a lesson," they said.

"It sure has," said the Little Manatee. "This is a lesson I will never forget!"

16

As the three of them swam off into the beautiful golden sunset, their hearts were full of happiness and peace because they were all together once again.

The end.

17

Draw anything you like.

Draw and color anything.

Notes

Made in the USA
Middletown, DE
03 May 2018